THE CREATURE FROM
MY CLOSET SERIES

"Original and hilarious." —*School Library Journal*

"Highly amusing . . . Skye gives Rob a self-deprecating
charm and highlights the pleasures of books both
subtly and effectively." —*Booklist*

"Rob's dry commentary on his family, school, and
social life is sure to provoke laughs."
—*Publishers Weekly*

"This pitch-perfect offering should appeal to
reluctant readers, not to mention the legion of Wimpy
Kid fans." —*Shelf Awareness*

BATNEEZER

THE CREATURE
FROM MY
CLOSET

OBERT SKYE

SQUARE
FISH

Christy Ottaviano Books

Henry Holt and Company ✦ New York

SQUARE
FISH

An imprint of Macmillan Publishing Group, LLC
175 Fifth Avenue, New York, NY 10010
mackids.com

Our books may be purchased in bulk for promotional, educational, or business use. Please contact
your local bookseller or the Macmillan Corporate and Premium Sales Department at
(800) 221-7945 ext. 5442 or by e-mail at MacmillanSpecialMarkets@macmillan.com.

Library of Congress Cataloging-in-Publication Data
Names: Skye, Obert, author, illustrator.
Title: Batneezer / Obert Skye.
Description: New York : Christy Ottaviano Books/Henry Holt and Company, 2016. | Series:
The creature from my closet ; 6 | Summary: "A strange combination of Ebenezer Scrooge
and Lego Batman helps Rob Burnside save his school"—Provided by publisher.
Identifiers: LCCN 2016008982 (print) | LCCN 2016028419 (ebook) | ISBN 9781250177223
(paperback) | ISBN 9781627798631 (Ebook)
Subjects: | CYAC: Middle schools—Fiction. | Schools—Fiction. | Monsters—Fiction. |
Humorous stories. | BISAC: JUVENILE FICTION / Humorous Stories. | JUVENILE FICTION /
Social Issues / Friendship. | JUVENILE FICTION / Books & Libraries.
Classification: LCC PZ7.S62877 Bat 2016 (print) | LCC PZ7.S62877 (ebook) | DDC [Fic]—dc23
LC record available at https://lccn.loc.gov/2016008982

Originally published in the United States by Christy Ottaviano Books/Henry Holt and Company
First Square Fish edition, 2018
Square Fish logo designed by Filomena Tuosto

1   3   5   7   9   10   8   6   4   2

AR: 4.6 / LEXILE: 830L

To Anodyne, Hagan, Sonora & Willow—
Four Amazing Human Beings

CONTENTS

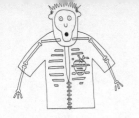

CHAPTER 1

ANTICIPATION

To begin with, Seussol is gone. There is no doubt about that. I saw him return to the closet over a month ago with my own eyes. And according to Beardy, my doorknob, he is gone for good. I miss my last visitor.

YOU MISSED ME.

I JUST SAID THAT.

ALSO YOU'RE NOT A VERY GOOD THROWER.

I am sad he's gone, but I'm also excited because it's December 21st, and that means there are only three more days before my closet opens again and the next creature arrives. I never had a heads-up in the past. All five of the creatures who came before were a surprise. But now, thanks to a tool Seussol made me, I'm able to unlock Beardy and see the date of the next arrival. Most people are pumped for the twenty-fifth. Me, I'm stoked for the twenty-fourth.

I'm actually happy about a lot of things right now. It's not often that I think my life is perfect, but at this exact moment, it's pretty close to that. For starters, I'm psyched that winter break begins in two days.

I love winter break—two weeks off from school and a couple of holidays mixed in. I'm also happy that Christmas is so close. I'm hopeful I might get some of the things I asked for this year.

Thanks to my closet, my life has become weird and unpredictable, and I have to admit I've grown to like the interruptions.

I'm kind of an average height, and I'm sort of an average-looking guy. I have average grades and I'm an average basketball player, but my life is no longer what it used to be. Let me give you the scoop.

My name is Robert Columbo Burnside. I have an older sister named Libby, a younger brother named Tuffin, and a mom and a dad. I have a fat dog named Puck and a pooping bird named Fred. I live on a street near a cul-de-sac. In the center of the cul-de-sac, there is a rock island with three palm trees growing in the middle of it. I have five friends who live in the cul-de-sac, and I hang out with them all the time.

The girl I like lives next door to me. Her name is Janae, and recently we've been getting along great. I mean, really great. She's even admitted to others without being forced that I'm her boyfriend.

YOU DON'T HAVE TO PINCH ME. ROB'S MY BOYFRIEND.

OBVIOUSLY THERE'S SOMETHING WRONG WITH YOU.

If you don't already know about my closet, I'll quickly fill you in. When I was little, it had no door and I created a homemade laboratory inside it. It was like my science cave. I would mix mayonnaise and motor oil and spread them over things in an attempt to find a cure for stuff like Older-Sister-Itis.

My potions never really worked. So I stopped trying to invent things, and my closet just got messier and goopier. Then my mom got a part-time job working in a bookstore. She said it was because she wanted to have something to do, but we all knew it was because she had three kids and wanted to get out of the house. She didn't work at the bookstore for too long, but while she did, she would bring home books for us all to read. I didn't like reading, so I would just take my books and throw them into my messy closet. I was pretty proud of how disgusting the inside of my closet was.

But then things changed.

THING

My dad found a strange door at a garage sale down the street. He brought it home and hung it on my closet. It's weird because it fit perfectly. It's also weird because it's . . . weird. It's a super-heavy closet door that looks older than dirt. It has an embarrassing unicorn sticker on it that I can't get off and a funny metal doorknob. On the front of the doorknob there's an engraved face of a bearded man I call Beardy.

His real name is Bartholomew, but if you read *Lord of the Hat*, you already knew that. Anyhow, soon after the closet door was installed, magical things began to happen. Beardy would lock the door and wouldn't let me or my friends in. Then the books and the mess behind the door would tumble and mix with the sticky lab supplies and create mashed-up characters.

Beardy is the gatekeeper of the closet and seems to be in control of who gets in and out. He doesn't talk, but on more than one occasion, he has rolled his eyes or made faces at me. He used to make me uncomfortable because he always seemed to be staring at me.

He doesn't make me nervous anymore. Now that I've learned where Beardy came from and how important he is, I feel privileged to have such an important doorknob.

When I first began writing down and drawing my experiences, I didn't like to read very much. Books used to be something for other people, but not me. Now, five creatures later, I catch myself reading just for the fun of it.

My closet has made me above average in the odd department. Only me and my five friends know what my closet can do with *books.* I've thought about telling Janae, but it seems like something I should wait to share when our relationship is stronger.

So my closet is a secret few people know about, and I'm okay with that. I like what it's done so far, and I'm *beside* myself with excitement knowing that in three days the door will unlock and I will find out who's next.

CHAPTER 2

MOURNING

I am not a morning person—I'm an afternoon human. Early risers like to wake up and pretend as if the sunrise is some amazing movie that they get to watch.

There's something suspicious about people who enjoy getting out of bed early. My first-period teacher, Ms. Welt, is suspicious. She loves mornings, and she takes every chance she gets to tell us that.

She's way different than my second-period teacher, Mr. Dunnell.

My dad likes mornings. He used to wake us up really early just so we could fill our lungs with what he called . . .

My mom doesn't like mornings. In fact, she doesn't really enjoy waking up before noon. A perfect day for her is one spent on the couch sleeping. I used to want her to get up more, but now that I'm older, I kind of like when she's napping. I never have to ask for permission to go out, and I never get assigned to do extra jobs. All I have to do is just stand there and whisper what I want. Then when she wakes up and questions what I've done, I just tell her that I already asked her permission.

One of the biggest reasons why I don't like mornings is because I like sleep. Sadly, however, my days of sleeping in are over. It hurts my heart just to say that, but my dad is determined to destroy my slumber. It started two weeks ago when he came home holding a present and wearing a scary grin.

When I opened the box there was nothing inside. I tipped it over and looked at the bottom—no clues or hints, just an empty box. I figured my dad was just giving me some air because he loved things like air and breathing. But what he actually was giving me was horrible.

WHAT IS IT?

IT'S A... PAPER ROUTE! THE EMPTY BOX IS JUST TO MAKE IT EXCITING!

My dad had gone behind my back and signed me up for an early-morning paper route. He actually thought it sounded fun for him to drive the car around while I threw papers. So now every morning for the last two weeks, I've had to get up and deliver newspapers with my dad. He is much too happy to begin with, and he is even worse in the mornings.

The first morning we did it was awful. It was cold and dark, and he kept reading me fun facts from the newspapers as I folded them. He would also tell me stories about how his dad used to give him their old newspapers to make hats with when he was a kid. I guess that was something people did for fun before smartphones were invented. Personally, I couldn't believe people still subscribed to newspapers.

Every morning, we got up at five and folded two hundred newspapers. We slipped coupons and ads into the middle and put a rubber band around the whole thing. I probably would have felt a little better if our city's paper actually had something good in it. But it was not a good paper.

After we folded and prepped the papers, my dad would drive us around and I'd toss them out the window while he said encouraging things.

NICE THROW! | TRY HITTING THE PORCH THIS TIME. | HOPEFULLY THAT DOG WILL BE OKAY.

Another problem with the paper route was that my dad thought it was a good time to ask a lot of painful questions.

DO YOU HAVE A CERTAIN LADY YOU LIKE? | HOW'S YOUR PERSONAL HYGIENE? | DO YOU KNOW HOW TO SHOWER PROPERLY?

But the worst thing about having a paper route and getting up early was Mrs. Penny Gwinn. I know it's not nice to say that, but even more awful than having to get up at five or fold a bunch of papers or having my dad tell me uncomfortable things was having to deliver newspapers to her. You

Know how some people are nice and some people are mean? Well, Mrs. Gwinn is the meanest. She's ornery, loud, and, well, let's just say she's worse than a butt load of splinters from a dry wooden bench.

She is also the tenth house up the street and on our paper route.

CHAPTER 3

SOGGY NEWS

Mrs. Penny Gwinn is horrible. I like old people, but she is old plus a bunch of other nasty things. She always has curlers in her gray hair. Her one talent seems to be complaining about everything, everyone, and every kid.

CHILDREN RUIN EVERYTHING. IN MY DAY, KIDS DIDN'T EVEN EXIST.

All she does is sit on her front porch under her shade umbrella and throw rocks at kids who are crazy enough to cut across her lawn. Jack has been pelted by her dozens of times.

WHERE HAVE YOU BEEN?

CROSSING GWINN'S LAWN.

Her voice sounds like glass cracking into a microphone, and she has deep-set eyes that give me the willies. She always wears a green housecoat that looks like a tent. She would be the perfect villain in any horror movie or comic.

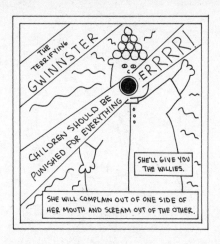

After we deliver her paper, she calls my mom and complains about the paper not being folded properly, or about it being thrown in the wrong spot, or that the news in the paper is too depressing.

She's bad enough on a normal day, but this morning I accidentally threw her paper into her birdbath.

When she found her paper soaking in water, she stormed directly to my house and demanded that I make things right. But when I offered to give her another newspaper, she said that wasn't enough. When my dad offered to pay her for the ruined newspaper, she said that wasn't enough either. And when my mom asked her what we could do to make things right, she said,

My parents and I just stared at her until my dad said he needed to go and ran off toward the

kitchen. I kept staring. I had no idea what her

boxes had to do with anything. So what if

Mrs. Gwinn had some things to move? She seemed

strong enough to lift an elephant. Certainly she

could handle a few boxes.

I started to laugh and then stopped when I

realized that she wasn't joking. I thought my mom

might laugh too, or tell her to just leave. But my

mom said something far worse.

I didn't know parents were allowed to make their children move things for other people. I knew they could make me unload our dishwasher or clean our cars, but were my parents allowed to hire me out to scary-looking women who smell a little like stinky cheese? Mrs. Gwinn threw out some instructions.

IT'S JUST A FEW BOXES, BUT IF YOUR BOY WILL HAUL THEM UP FROM MY BASEMENT, I MIGHT FORGET ABOUT HIM DESTROYING MY NEWSPAPER.

THAT SOUNDS FAIR.

I love my parents, but they have no idea what fair is. My mom promised Mrs. Gwinn that I'd be over after school to help move her boxes. Mrs. Gwinn looked at me with her angry eyes, sniffed at me with her tiny nose, and then turned and marched off. I shivered. There was no way I

was going into her house. As soon as she was gone,
I began my argument.

My mom wouldn't back down. She thought it
would be good for me to help out an old woman. I
wanted to point out to my mother that it wasn't
even my fault—my dad had told me to throw the
paper, and my dad had made me have the paper
route in the first place. I wanted to state my case,
but at that moment, the school bus pulled up in
front of our house and I had to run and catch it. I
was not happy about what was happening, but I

knew that if I missed the bus, it wouldn't help anything. When I got to school, I was in a foul mood. In fact, all day long I stewed over the Mrs. Gwinn situation.

Right before lunch, I ran into Principal Smelt in the hallway. I usually tried to avoid him, but my mind was preoccupied and I didn't see him until it was too late.

I had not met Mr. Kerr, but I knew exactly who he was. That's because EVERYONE at my school knew who he was. He had a really bushy goatee and a bad wig that didn't sit right on his head. For the last couple of weeks, all Principal Smelt could talk about was Mr. Kerr and how he was going to remodel our school library because apparently we needed an upgrade. According to Principal Smelt, Mr. Kerr was going to give us . . .

THE MOST BEAUTIFUL STATE-OF-THE-ART MEDIA CENTER THIS TOWN HAS EVER SEEN.

Our school had won a contest that Mr. Kerr's company was running, and now we were getting a library overhaul. According to Principal Smelt, we were soon going to have the kind of media center that would . . .

Mr. Kerr had been hanging around our school for a while, getting things ready. He had even moved his camper into the middle of our school parking lot so that he could easily work and sleep and be close to the school.

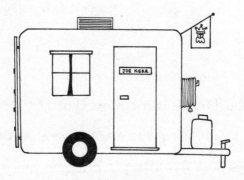

His camper was small, but he claimed it had everything he needed.

I didn't really care about keys, or Mr. Kerr, or campers. In fact, I was kind of bothered by the guy. He had shifty eyes and laughed like a cartoon villain whenever Principal Smelt told a joke. Besides, our library was fine as it was. A lot of the books I had read recently had come from there. Now an outsider had come in to make things "better."

Principal Smelt told a joke, and Mr. Kerr laughed. I couldn't stand the sound, so I excused myself from the conversation and left.

Also, it was lunchtime and I was hungry.

I ate my food sitting on the wall outside of the

cafeteria with my friends. Janae walked by right
after I took a big bite of my sandwich.

When she walked off, my friends began to make
fun of me like they sometimes did. Actually, they
made fun of me like they usually did. To be honest,
they made fun of me like it was their destiny.

Trevor was my only friend who didn't give me grief. Maybe it was because he was too dorky to know how to make fun of me, or maybe it was because he really was a good guy. I think it's probably because he's dorky. Oddly enough, I think Trevor would probably agree with me.

Trevor reminded me that I had something very important to ask my friends. So I swallowed my food and spoke.

CHAPTER 4

NOT SO PLEASANT

I have *been* taught my whole life not to be selfish,
so I decided to invite my friends to help me move
boxes at Mrs. Gwinn's after school. I knew that if I
could get one of them to come with me, it would go
faster and be way less boring. They all wanted to
know what I would pay them to help. Well, everyone
besides Trevor.

OKAY, I'LL GO. I NEED A
COUPLE MORE HOURS OF
COMMUNITY SERVICE TO
EARN MY NEW PLEASANT PIN.

Trevor is a Pleasant Scout. He is a member of troop number *Friendly Wave*. I know *Friendly Wave* isn't actually a number, but not much about the Pleasant Scouts makes sense. They meet once a month and work on doing things that Trevor always says are . . .

WILDLY PLEASANT!

One month, they lowered the slides at the park so that they weren't so steep. Another time, they went on a trip to a hotel where they gave the maids a rest and cleaned their own hotel rooms. The leader of the Pleasant Scouts is a man named Rick. He has a bald head and always wears the official Pleasant Scout neckwear and vest.

The motto of the Pleasant Scouts is *It doesn't take a hero to wave*. They even have a pledge, which Trevor has told me on a number of occasions. Just last week when I was thinking of keeping a pencil I found in the school parking lot, he recited it for me again. It was sort of painful to hear, and the worst part was that he always marched in place when he recited it.

A PLEASANT SCOUT IS...
AGREEABLE, ENJOYABLE, ACCEPTABLE, AMIABLE, POLITE, FAIR, WE GIVE A CARE. WE ARE ALSO AFFABLE, LAUGHABLE, BLAND, CIVILIZED, HANDY, DANDY, BUT NOT TOO DANDY, OBLIGING, REFRESHING, AND LIKABLE.

WHAT DOES THAT HAVE TO DO WITH ME KEEPING THIS PENCIL?

I'M NOT SURE WHAT AFFABLE MEANS. IT MIGHT MEAN NOT KEEPING THINGS THAT ARENT YOURS. BUT PROBABLY NOT.

At the moment, I was fine with Trevor being a Pleasant Scout. I was more than happy to help him earn another Pleasant Pin if it meant he would be helping me move boxes. Jack also wanted to come. He had heard there was a dead body in Mrs. Gwinn's basement, and he wanted to check it out for himself.

YOU KNOW, JUST POKE AROUND. MAYBE ASK A FEW QUESTIONS.

I was okay with that too. I figured either we would get all the boxes moved quickly or we would bug Mrs. Gwinn so much that she would insist that we leave and never come back. My other three friends didn't want to help. Actually, Rourk wanted to come and . . .

JUST WATCH YOU WORK.

But even when Rourk was helping, he was horrible. So I told him that there was a two-friend limit.

THERE'S ALWAYS A FRIEND LIMIT WHEN I WANT TO COME.

After school Trevor, Jack, and I all walked up the street to Mrs. Gwinn's house. I was feeling a little better knowing that I would have some friends to help me. Sadly, Mrs. Gwinn didn't feel the same.

NO FRIENDS! THIS IS A HOME, NOT A JUVENILE DETENTION CENTER.

CAN I JUST COME IN AND LOOK AROUND?

Mrs. Gwinn picked up Jack by the back of his shirt and pushed him away from her house. Trevor figured a hug might make her feel differently about letting him stay, but when he moved in, she thought he was attacking her, so she swatted him with a long, lacy pillow she had on her porch. I guess the swatting changed Trevor's mind.

My coward friends took off running down the street and left me alone with Mrs. Gwinn.

After only two minutes inside Mrs. Gwinn's smelly house, here's what I learned. One: she grunts a lot when she walks. I know this because I had to listen to her make noises that most animals would be embarrassed to have associated with them.

The second thing I learned about her was when she says "move a few boxes upstairs," what she really means is "move hundreds of boxes filled with heavy books up a tall, thin set of rickety steps."

There were so many boxes in her basement.

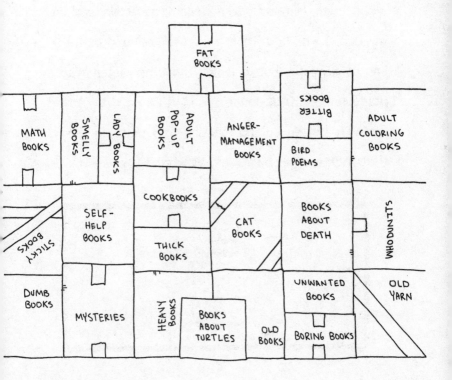

I started the afternoon liking books. I ended the afternoon with a sore back and being mad at them. When it reached seven o'clock, I wasn't even halfway done, but the Gwinnster stopped me and handed me a note for my mother and then told me I could go. I took the envelope and ran from the house. I didn't stop running until I reached my bedroom window. I slid it open, climbed into my room, and collapsed on my bed. I was beat, bothered, bruised, and at the end of my rope. But at least I had the winter break party tomorrow at Janae's to look forward to. And it was way better looking forward to something like that than looking backward at what I'd just left.

THE OBJECT IN THE MIRROR IS MEANER THAN IT APPEARS

CHAPTER 5

~

UNJUSTLY PUNISHED

I had been lying on my bed for only two minutes when Libby stuck her big head in my bedroom and yelled,

MOM! HE'S IN HERE!

Ten seconds later, my mother was in my room questioning me about Mrs. Gwinn. She was curious to know what went on in her house. So I told her the truth and nothing but the truth.

IT WAS HORRIBLE, FRIGHTENING, TERRIBLE, TRAGIC, SCARY, AND THE WORST! OH, AND HER CARPETS ARE STICKY AND HER HOME IS COLD AND SMELLS LIKE TUFFIN'S SOCKS AFTER A VERY HOT AND SWEATY DAY.

I handed my mom the note Mrs. Gwinn had given me. I figured it was a card to thank me and let me know that I was forgiven for the soggy newspaper. My mother opened the envelope and read the note aloud.

MRS. BURNSIDE,
YOUR SON WASN'T QUICK ENOUGH TO FINISH THE JOB. HE WILL NEED TO RETURN TOMORROW. I WILL BE EXPECTING HIM RIGHT AFTER SCHOOL. HE HAD BETTER WORK HARDER THAN HE DID TODAY.
MRS. G

P.S. MY NEWSPAPER BETTER NOT BE WET TOMORROW MORNING.

I couldn't *believe* it. It would take hours to move the rest of those boxes. Besides, I couldn't go back the next day, *because* it was Janae's winter break party. The Gwinnster would have to wait.

I told my mom about Janae's party and how important it was for me to show up, but she still wouldn't back down. She thought the most important thing a young man could do was carry boxes of books that no one was ever going to read upstairs while missing out on the social event of the season.

My mom didn't like the way I was talking. I should have played it cool. I should have just kept my mouth shut and waited until she was napping to ask permission to skip out on Mrs. Gwinn and go to Janae's tomorrow. I know all that, but for some reason, I kept saying things that were making the situation even messier.

I had gone too far. The after-school party was slipping away. I saw myself having to spend my whole break moving boxes. I saw my friends having fun and me being surrounded by nothing but bad smells and books. I'd thought books were good, but they were turning out to be bad.

I was getting really upset with my mom. It wasn't like me to do so, but I was doing so. Sometimes middle-school students don't know how to feel. We're funny that way. I want to be a nice person others like to be around, but then sometimes I act like a real wedge. Which is what Jack calls people he thinks are dumb.

Nudge is what Trevor calls people because he thinks wedge sounds too mean. The point is that sometimes I act nudgelike, but it's not because I want to. My mind is just being stubborn.

I feel like I've grown up a lot in the last six months. My closet has been a big part of that, but I'm also halfway done with my last year of middle school. Things are changing. Even my friends are changing. Teddy is taller than ever. Aaron's voice is super deep now, and every lie he tells sounds serious and like an old man is saying it.

I HAVE THE ABILITY TO FLY.

MY PANTS ARE BULLETPROOF.

I ONCE ATE TEN WHOLE CHICKENS, FEATHERS AND ALL.

I BELIEVE YOU BECAUSE YOU SOUND SERIOUS.

ALSO, THE GOVERNMENT WANTS TO HIRE ME TO SOLVE ALL ITS PROBLEMS.

Rourk sweats more than he used to, and Jack... is the same. Trevor also seems a little different. He now wears jeans with weird things and dumb words on the back pockets because, as he puts it,

THEY MAKE MY REAR LOOK COOL.

THEY MAKE ME NOT WANT TO STAND ANYWHERE NEAR YOU.

Things are changing. I'm growing up, I even have a sort-of girlfriend. What I'm trying to say is that I don't want to act stubborn, but because I'm getting older, I'm having a hard time keeping my mouth shut. And right then, the more I kept talking, the more determined my mother was to ruin my life.

I wanted to storm off and slam my door, but we were in my room, so I had to wait for my mom to walk out and then shut the door behind her. I was pretty upset. I shook my head, wondering what was going on with my life. I looked at Beardy and growled.

Beardy looked offended—bad-talking books was not something he was fond of. I thought about saying sorry, but I was still too mad. Besides, I always felt stupid apologizing to my doorknob.

When my dad came home that evening, I tried to win him over in an effort to get him to change my mom's mind about tomorrow. But as usual, he was on my mom's side. When I told him that he was partly to blame for all of this because he was the one who got the paper route, he said,

I begged him to understand how important Janae's winter break party was to my social well-being. I reasoned with him about how I needed to be true to my word and show up at the gathering.

I explained my feelings of how I knew deep in my soul that the party was the right thing to do. I offered to move boxes for Mrs. Gwinn on Saturday. I laid out every excuse and reason I could think of, but in the end he said,

AHHHHHHHH! Okay, if you're an adult reading this, you should know that kids hate hearing things like that. It's not like this was the end of some epic movie and my dad was handing me a glowing sword to chop apart a bunch of enchanted teacups for my mom.

No, this was my life, and my dad was handing me some line about how I should forget everything I wanted to do and instead do what my mom "kind of" wanted me to do. Well, I "really" wanted to hang out with Janae, and what was happening seemed completely unfair.

After dinner, I climbed out my window to go to the rock island in the cul-de-sac. My friends were there comparing feet and arguing about whose were the biggest.

I told them to stop acting like babies and then started to whine about how my parents weren't going to let me go to Janae's tomorrow afternoon. I suggested that maybe all of them should skip the party and come help me move boxes. I tried to make it sound like Mrs. Gwinn's house was fun, but there wasn't much I could think of.

They weren't interested in warm tap water. They were, however, pretty interested in making me feel even more horrible about not being able to go to the party.

IT'S GOING TO BE GREAT. THERE'LL BE OVER FIVE GIRLS THERE!

I couldn't stand hearing what they were saying, so I left the island and returned home. I didn't know why the universe hated me at the moment, but I felt picked on. I also felt bummed out. In fact, in the history of time, I don't think there had ever been anyone sadder than me.

SIGH.

OH, BOTHER.

I'M THE WORST.

YOU GUYS LOOK HAPPY TO ME.

SAD   SADDER   SADDEST   ME

CHAPTER 6

TOTALLY CREAKY

Friday morning, my father woke me up *so that* we could hit the paper route. If my bad luck kept going, I would probably mess up again and have to spend my entire winter break cleaning someone's sewer or repairing a toilet.

THIS IS HORRIBLE.

WELL, THEN YOU SHOULDN'T HAVE THROWN MY PAPER ON THE WRONG PART OF MY LAWN.

I couldn't believe how sore and out of sorts I was because of Mrs. Gwinn and her stupid books. As I folded the papers to get them ready, I was mad. When we got in the car and began driving around the neighborhood, I was steaming. And when we got to Mrs. Gwinn's house, I was scared. Instead of throwing her paper, I took it up to the porch and rested it nicely against the door. There was no way she could complain about that. My dad was impressed.

I LIKE TO SEE MY BOY GOING THE EXTRA MILE.

I tried using the positive energy to talk my dad into letting me off the hook. I wanted him to tell me that I could go to Janae's party. I wanted him to tell me that he and my mom had been wrong and that I was a perfect kid who didn't need to help Mrs. Gwinn move a single book. So I asked him nicely if he and my mom would please change their minds, and he replied,

NO, THANK YOU.

When I got to school, we had an assembly during
first period. It wasn't a great assembly. It was just
a chance for Mr. Kerr to go on and on about what a
wonderful new library we were going to have. He
told the crowd that it would be remodeled over
winter break, and when we came back to school in
two weeks, we would all be blown away by how
beautiful it was. At that point in the assembly, Jack
decided to yell,

IF YOU LOVE THE
LIBRARY SO MUCH,
WHY DON'T YOU
MARRY IT?

Everyone laughed, but Mr. Kerr didn't seem
bothered. He just moved his mouth closer to the
microphone and said very seriously,

When the library is done, everyone here will want to marry it.

I think he was hoping we'd all laugh, but nobody did. So he said a few more things about how much he loved libraries, and then he laughed his evil laugh and sat down. The assembly ended with Principal Smelt and his band, Leftover Angst, singing a new song they had written about our librarian, Mrs. Lip.

And we're proud to have
a librarian.
She's the best that
she can be.
And we won't forget
the books she orders,
books for both
you and me.
And we'll gladly
read them every week,
and enjoy them every day.
Because there ain't no
doubt we love this place
please bless our library!

I kept trying to think of a way to get out of going to Mrs. Gwinn's. I couldn't act sick because then I wouldn't be allowed to go to the party. I couldn't just skip out on Mrs. Gwinn because she would call my mom to see where I was and then I'd be in even more trouble. I couldn't ask Janae to postpone her party because, well . . .

HEY, DO YOU THINK I COULD ASK JANAE TO POSTPONE HER PARTY?

IF YOU WANT HER TO HATE YOU.

I should have felt good when the last bell rang. School was out for the next two weeks. My heart should have been filled with nothing but happiness. Instead, it was filled with things far less joyful.

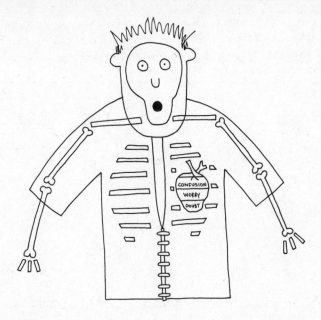

Right after I got home, I ran to Mrs. Gwinn's house. I wanted to make one last attempt to get out of moving boxes. I was going to be honest with her. Beneath her rough exterior, there had to be a person who could sympathize with my problem. I would appeal to her human side. I would speak my heart, and she would be so moved that she'd let me go and give me twenty dollars to spend on snacks to bring. I rang her doorbell. The moment she opened up, I stated my case.

After I was done speaking, I took a second to catch my breath. Mrs. Gwinn stared at me until I felt so uncomfortable that I started to sweat. Finally, she opened her mouth and said,

I couldn't believe it. I had poured my heart out, and she didn't care. Mrs. Gwinn had no soul, no kindness, and no humanity.

It was bad enough having to carry all those books up the stairs. But what made it even worse was thinking about the things my friends were doing now at Janae's. Each box of books I carried made me madder and madder and sadder and sadder. It felt like the whole world was out to get me: Mrs. Gwinn, my parents, books, my friends. I couldn't see how anyone thought this was fair. Why didn't my friends have my back?

Why didn't they come help me? I would have helped them. I would never have left my friends to work alone. Okay, sure, three weeks ago, I didn't help Trevor when he had to clean out his garage, but that was different. I was busy listening to music in my room. And it's true that I decided to skip out on helping Jack clean his gutters, but I couldn't make it because there was a show I had DVRed that I had been wanting to watch for almost a month. So maybe I should have been a better friend, but cleaning garages and gutters is nothing like having to miss a party while working for the Gwinn.

After I was halfway done bringing boxes upstairs, Mrs. Gwinn told me to start unloading some of the books onto the empty bookcases.

MY MOM SAID I'M ONLY ALLOWED TO CARRY THE BOXES. I'M NOT RESPONSIBLE ENOUGH TO UNLOAD THEM.

WELL, IF YOU STOP YOUR WHINING AND FILL TWO BOOKCASES, YOU CAN LEAVE AT SIX INSTEAD OF SEVEN.

If I left at six, I would be able to go to the last hour of Janae's party. I could walk in like a working man, and everyone would be super impressed.

SORRY I'M LATE, BABE. I HAD TO EARN ME SOME DOUGH.

OH, ROB, YOU'RE SO EMPLOYABLE.

I excitedly carried boxes up the stairs as quickly as I could. I got one bookcase filled and was working on the second when I heard an uncomfortable creaking noise. I looked around, wondering what it was. I checked the clock on the wall. It was five minutes to six, and I had the second bookcase almost filled. My back was sore, my legs were tired, and my stomach felt like a big wad of worry. Plus, my hands and body were completely dirty due to the dusty boxes and old books I had been handling. I continued to put the last books onto the shelf, marveling at some of the awful titles.

It was clear that Mrs. Gwinn's home library was going to be as mean and angry as she was. The only book I saw of hers that had any interest to me was one that mentioned the Thumb Buddies—the small thumbtack characters that I secretly collect.

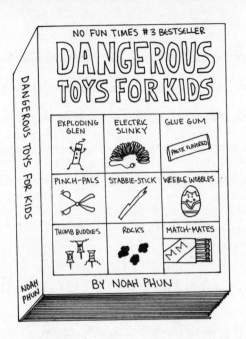

NO FUN TIMES #3 BESTSELLER

DANGEROUS TOYS FOR KIDS

EXPLODING GLEN	ELECTRIC SLINKY	GLUE GUM
		PASTE FLAVORED
PINCH-PALS	STABBIE-STICK	WEEBLE WOBBLES
THUMB BUDDIES	ROCKS	MATCH-MATES

BY NOAH PHUN

But even that *book* was mean-spirited, and it only had two pages on the Thumb Buddies and no information that I didn't already know. I filled up another shelf, and again I heard the noise.

For a second, I thought it might be the sound of some new creature. It was not unlike my closet to set things loose in a secretive fashion—Katfish had hunted me down; Seussol had stowed away. But I knew that today was the twenty-third of December, and according to the date I saw when I unlocked Beardy, I wasn't supposed to get my next visitor until tomorrow, the twenty-fourth.

CREEEEEAK!

The sound was louder now. I hollered out for Mrs. Gwinn. I knew from experience that sometimes she made weird noises, and I figured it could easily be her.

If it was her, she wasn't here to admit it. I put some more books on the shelf and glanced around nervously.

CREEEEEEEEEAK!

I shelved the last book and twisted to get up off my knees and out of Mrs. Gwinn's creepy house. As I was turning, the noise screamed again, but this time my eyes could see exactly where it was coming from. . . .

WHAT'S GOING ON?

HOLD ON—I'LL SHOW YOU.

CHAPTER 7

BENT

The first bookcase was pulling away from the wall and falling DIRECTLY TOWARD ME!

Before I could move out of the way, the bookcase and all its books crashed down on me. The crash caused the second bookshelf to wobble and fall too. I couldn't move because my legs were tucked underneath me. The books might have protected me from the shelves, but now I was pinned by piles of words and paper.

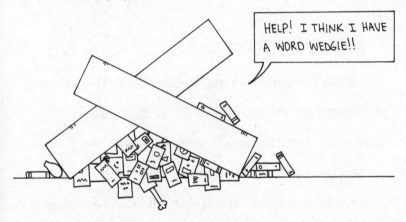

HELP! I THINK I HAVE A WORD WEDGIE!!

I tried yelling louder and longer, but still no response. I knew Mrs. Gwinn was in the house, because there was no way she would leave me alone with her stuff. But for some reason, she wasn't answering my cries for help.

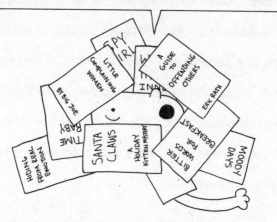

It wasn't the most urgent situation, but I was stuck, and I needed to get to the party. All of that didn't matter, however, because as loud as I screamed, nobody came. I tried to wiggle and thrash my way out, but no luck. From where I was buried, I could see that her fruit-themed wall clock said it was already five after six.

I didn't have any time to mess around, but the clock kept ticking and I was still stuck. At six thirty, I started to panic. And by a quarter to seven, I felt hopeless. What had I been thinking? I *knew* books were bad! I knew it! The creatures that had come out had tricked me into thinking *books* would make things better. I was a fool! This was probably the plan the whole time. The creatures had worked me over, and the second I let my guard down, they attacked me with *books* and were teaching me one last lesson.

When the clock struck seven, I gave up all hope. Not because I thought I was going to die—I mean, I knew my parents would come looking for me eventually, because they had other things they wanted to punish me for. I knew I'd live, but I had no hope for Janae's. The party was over, and I had been a no-show.

I really needed to move my right arm, because my rear end itched and I couldn't reach it. I tried to scrunch my buns together to see if that would help, but it didn't. Finally, I heard Mrs. Gwinn. She came into the room and acted like I had made the mess on purpose.

I explained that I didn't mean to get buried. I also informed her that I had been trapped for over an hour.

It took a few minutes for her to pull the bookshelves off me. Then she shoved some books like a bulldozer, and I was able to flip over onto my hands and knees and eventually stand. My legs were kind of asleep, and I wobbled like a dying top.

Mrs. Gwinn was not happy about what had happened. She felt bad for her shelves and was ready for me to go. She could also see that there was no way I was ever coming back.

She didn't say thanks. She just slammed the door as I walked away. My whole body ached. I was also dirty and sore. I felt pretty certain that I never wanted to see a book again.

As I walked past Janae's house on my way home, I could see the last of her guests leaving. They had huge smiles on their faces and were laughing like people who hadn't spent their evening buried under books. All five of my friends were already on the island discussing the night.

It didn't surprise me that Janae had guessed that. Everyone knew Trevor was scared of chewed gum. One time, Jack had put a piece on Trevor's back, and he had spun around in a circle for fifteen minutes trying to get it off. Eventually, he had to run to his house, where his mom pulled it off while wearing rubber gloves.

Trevor's mom tried to ground Jack for doing the prank, but since Jack's parents couldn't really get him to behave, she had little success.

I told all my friends what had happened at Mrs. Gwinn's with the *bookshelves attacking me* and how I was lucky to be alive.

Unfortunately, they were probably right.

CHAPTER 8

DUBBED OUT

When I got home, I was too tired to climb through my window, so I went to the front door. It was locked. I rang the bell and Libby answered.

GO AWAY! WE DON'T WANT ANY.

I wasn't in the mood to insult her, so I pushed past and went to the kitchen for some food.

Mrs. Gwinn had only fed me a few dry crackers with tuna fish and a slice of cucumber and a dot of mustard on them.

GROSS MUSTARD
GROSS TUNA
GROSS CUCUMBER
GROSS CRACKER

They were awful, but that and tap water were all she gave me. I also had to eat them fast because she watched me and kept telling me to hurry.

STUFF YOUR FACE FASTER! YOU NEED TO GET BACK TO WORK.

I'M STUFFING, I'M STUFFING.

When I walked into our kitchen, I saw a bunch of wrappers on the table from Dubby Burger, my favorite fast-food restaurant.

I got excited. We never went to Dubby. The only Dubby restaurant was across town, so it was a rare treat to get to eat there. I looked around, searching for what they had gotten me, but the only things on the table were crumpled, EMPTY wrappers.

WE ARE CONTAINERS THAT HELD YOUR FOOD.

WE ARE HERE WITH AN ATTITUDE.

ONE OF US IS FOIL.

THE OTHER IS NOT.

WE KEEP YOUR FOOD FRESH AND HOT!

FOOD TO YOUR MOTHER!

PUFF DUBBY

FRIES

FOOD WRAPPERS

My heart *beat* with worry. I opened the refrigerator to *see* if my family had put my food in there to keep it fresh for me. No Dubby. I looked around the kitchen like a crazy person playing a desperate game of hamburger hide-and-seek. There was no Dubby anywhere! All I could *see* was Tuffin standing there with Dubby sauce all over his face and smiling in a way that only a Dubby Meal could make him smile.

MY STOMACH FEELS WARM AND FRIENDLY.

I ran to the family room, where my parents were sitting on the couch watching a reality show about a woman named Barbara Flant. She had died for two minutes, then miraculously came back to life. Now she could talk to plants. The show was called *Flant's Plants*.

I gladly interrupted the show to ask my parents where my food was. The food they had surely gotten for me when they went to Dubby Burger. The food I needed and deserved because I had spent the last two days missing out on things that mattered to me and moving heavy *boxes* for an old woman who made the Grinch seem kind of friendly.

I wanted the Dubby to make up for all the horrible things I had just been through. The food would usher in Christmas and bring about the miracle of me thinking things were going to be okay.

I stared at my parents in disbelief. Here's what I thought was going to happen.

This is what actually happened.

I was numb and defeated. Misunderstood and upset. At my wits' end. I slowly stumbled back into the kitchen and grabbed a full loaf of bread. I shuffled to my room, lay on my bed, and shoved pieces of white bread into my mouth. I rolled over and stared at Beardy. I had been so pumped for him to open up tomorrow, but now I couldn't imagine dealing with a new visitor. My head was tired and confused. I wanted nothing to do with what Beardy would be letting loose, and I was no longer thinking straight.

I found a chair and jammed it under Beardy to make sure he wouldn't be able to open the closet door.

Beardy looked sad, but I didn't care. I stuffed two more pieces of bread into my mouth and then changed into one of my dad's old concert shirts and went to bed early like an old, miserly shut-in.

CHAPTER 9

THE BEGINNING
OF A LONG NIGHT

At exactly midnight, my alarm clock rang, so I rolled over and turned it off. It was weird because I never set my alarm clock. Especially for twelve at night. I lay in my bed and looked up into the darkness. My room was quiet, which made it easy to close my eyes and start to fall back to sleep. But as I was hopping on the train to Sleepytown, something brushed over me. I reached up and scratched my nose. Then, as I rolled over onto my right side, I accidentally smashed the bag of bread I had been eating earlier. As I mushed it, air escaped from the sack, making a disgusting noise.

BLUNDER BREAD

BUURRRPT!

My eyelids sprang open and I stared into the dark. I pulled the smooshed bread out from under me and flung it toward my closet. It hit the door and fell to the floor. I would have been asleep in the next few seconds, but I heard a click. Goose pimples ran up and down my arms and legs.

WHAT'S HAPPENING?

I was pretty certain that the bread hadn't made the clicking noises. Besides, the click sounded familiar. I thought about getting up and turning on my light, but I didn't want anything to reach out from under my bed and grab my ankles.

- CLICK
CLICK
- CLICK -

My brain woke up fully and began to holler at me about what I should be thinking.

IT'S GOT TO BE YOUR CLOSET!!

But Beardy wasn't glowing, and it was too dark to see my closet door. I reached into the small drawer on my nightstand and pulled out the tiny flashlight I had won at school for guessing the number of the day correctly. It was a dumb thing that Principal Smelt did. He would call in ten students and have them guess the number of the day. If you got it right, or if you were closest, he would give you a sticker or a paper hat or a tiny flashlight. I had been called in last week, and I had guessed . . .

The answer was thirty, and I won the flashlight. It was plastic and so cheap that it only shone a little beam of light. I pushed the button to turn it on and directed the light toward the closet door. It looked normal, with the chair still wedged up under Beardy.

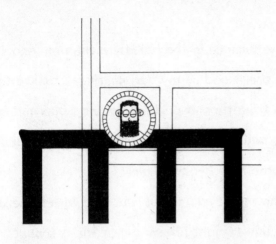

I moved the light around my room. Nothing was out of place. So I switched off the flashlight and set it on top of my nightstand. I tried to get my brain to settle down and go back to sleep, which wasn't easy to do, because it was pretty amped up.

I NEED TO PUNCH SOMETHING!

The furnace in the hallway kicked on, and I could hear the sound of my dad snoring. I took a few deep breaths and pushed my head back into my pillow while trying to relax the rest of my body.

Something began to glow.

I had my eyelids shut, but I could tell there was something bright hovering over me. I thought that maybe I had fallen back to sleep and was dreaming. I didn't want to open my eyes, but my brain needed to see what was going on.

COME ON, WE'VE GOT TO CHECK THIS OUT.

I opened my right eyelid and gasped. What I saw startled me so much that my left eyelid sprang open without permission. I yelped and put my hands over my mouth to stop myself from screaming. There, hovering over me, was a headless ghost.

It was floating, its robe waving gently, holding its head in its arm. I looked over at my closet. The chair was still in place, but Beardy's eyes were open and glowing. He looked smug. I closed my eyes and pulled my blankets up.

Apparently I'm a liar, because when I opened my eyes again, the ghost was still there. He lifted his head and snapped it onto his neck.

The visitor was about the same size as me, but as he floated, his size seemed to expand and contract. Part of him appeared to be made out of LEGOs, and he was wearing a half robe. There was a portion of a bat painted on his chest, and he was wearing a stocking cap and a monocle like Mr. Peanut. I could see different shades of gray and white all over him as he glowed in the night.

He knew my full name and said it like I was in trouble. There was a chain rattling from his left arm.

That made *sense*. Actually, none of this made sense. What kind of person has a closet that sets alarms and spits out ghosts? I wanted to know exactly who I was talking to, so I said,

The ghost shivered and moved about. He snapped off his right arm and scratched his head, thinking. Just as the silence was becoming uncomfortable, he spoke.

It made sense that he liked those names. Alfred is Batman's butler, and I know the Scrooge book is

written by Charles Dickens because that was the
book we were reading in my language arts class.

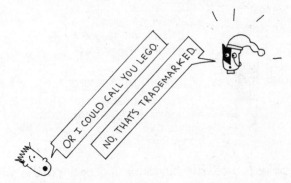

He thought for a moment and then decided that
he wanted to be called by Scrooge's first name,
Ebenezer. I suggested Batneezer, because it was a
combination of characters and because I have
always liked words with a z in them.

Thankfully he agreed. I watched Batneezer snap
his arm back on and float over to my window. He

tried to pull open the curtains, but because he was just a ghost, he couldn't.

WOULD YOU MIND OPENING THE WINDOW? IT'S A BIT STUFFY IN HERE.

I'M SORRY ABOUT THAT. TOO MUCH BREAD MAKES ME GASSY.

I pulled back the curtains and opened the window. A cool breeze drifted in, reminding me that it was winter in Temon. It never got very cold here, but there was a slight chill now, and the night was very dark. I quickly hopped back into my bed. Batneezer reached out his hands, and the chain on his left arm clanked. His other hand was yellow and plastic. When I asked him what the chain was for, he said,

IT WAS FORGED IN LIFE. IT REPRESENTS THE BOOKS I SHOULD HAVE READ. I'M HERE TO MAKE SURE THE SAME THING DOESN'T HAPPEN TO YOU.

I don't mean to be rude, but just once it would be nice if a creature from my closet gave me a chest of gold or a dirt bike. This one was here to bust me for not reading *enough books*. My feelings for books had improved a lot over the last year, but right now I felt differently.

SPEAK COMFORT TO ME, BATNEEZER. I'M SICK OF BOOKS AT THE MOMENT. I REALLY DON'T WANT TO SEE ANOTHER ONE.

Batneezer put his fingers in his ears. When he saw I was done talking, he removed his fingers and warned me about how troublesome life would be if I turned my back on books. I then took a moment to tell him how troublesome my life had become with them.

The bruise came from when I was fighting Libby for some cookies she found in the pantry, but Batneezer didn't need to know that. He drifted around my room, shaking his chain and clicking his LEGO bricks. He moaned about how I didn't know real trouble like the good people of Gotham did. He worked himself up and worked his way back over my bed.

I was worried about having to entertain a bunch of spirits or find a place for them to hide or sleep. It was hard enough keeping one creature hidden. Now I would have four? I had put the chair up against the closet door because I was mad at books. This seemed like it might turn out to be too much for me to handle. I told the ghost my concern, and he detached his right arm and scratched his forehead.

YOU MIGHT WANT TO GROW UP. I LOST MY PARENTS WHEN I WAS A KID. DO YOU SEE ME MOPING AROUND?

ACTUALLY, BATMAN DOES A LOT OF MOPING.

WHAT DO YOU EXPECT? I LOST MY PARENTS.

Batneezer took a moment to look sad. For some reason, ghosts aren't very scary when they look sad. I actually felt sorry for the Bruce Wayne part of my new visitor. As for the Scrooge part of him, I didn't know a ton about his story. I just knew he was a miserly cheapwad, so I didn't feel as bad for that part of him. After a few moments of silence, I asked the creature why he was here.

GOTHAM IS ASLEEP, ROB, AND WE HAVE COME TO SHOW YOU THINGS YOU HAVE NEVER SEEN.

LIKE A TWO-HEADED MAN?

NO.

THEN WHAT?

HAVE YOU READ THE BOOK A CHRISTMAS CAROL?

I'M READING IT. PLUS, I'VE SEEN THE CARTOON MOVIE.

Batneezer looked very disappointed. He rattled around the room, complaining about movies and how

kids were ungrateful when it came to books. He
sighed and then stretched his right arm toward me.

I reached out, hoping I was doing the right thing.

CHAPTER 10

SOMETHING IS ROTTEN

I took hold of Batneezer's garment sleeve, and instantly
the two of us began to float. I wanted to scream
again, but the sensation was so great, I kept my
mouth shut and tried to enjoy what was happening.
As I held on to his arm, we flew out the window and
up over to Janae's house. We drifted down the street
with Batneezer making a low moaning noise.

I really liked how this creature traveled. I had had to carry Wonkenstein and Potterwookiee in a backpack. Pinocula had gotten around by himself, Katfish had had to be toted in a wheelbarrow, and Seussol had come in our RV. Now my new visitor was flying me around.

THIS IS GREAT!

IT'S NOT AS COOL AS THE BATMOBILE.

We flew over houses and straight toward Softrock Middle School. When we got there, I could see that most of the lights were off. I could also see Mr. Kerr's camper sitting in the middle of the parking lot. We drifted down to the school and stood by the window that looked into the main office. Inside, standing next to the front counter and talking on a phone, was Mr. Kerr. It was midnight, and he was alone in my school. Something wasn't right. Batneezer instructed me to keep holding his sleeve as he pushed me up against the window. Like magic, we slipped through the glass and were standing right next to Mr. Kerr. I could hear everything he was saying.

Mr. Kerr laughed, said a few more mean things, and hung up the phone. He stretched and then turned and looked in our direction. He couldn't see us! When he reached to grab his briefcase on the counter, his hand went right through Batneezer. Mr. Kerr picked up his briefcase and walked out of the office. I was amazed, but I was also curious about what he had been doing.

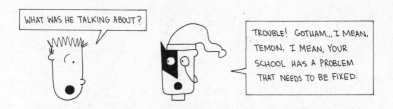

WHAT WAS HE TALKING ABOUT?

TROUBLE! GOTHAM... I MEAN, TEMON, I MEAN, YOUR SCHOOL HAS A PROBLEM THAT NEEDS TO BE FIXED.

Batneezer told me to hold on tight, and we flew up through the roof and into the night sky. When we arrived at my house, he pulled me through my window and dropped me on my beanbag.

I DON'T UNDERSTAND WHAT'S GOING ON WITH MR. KERR.

JUST KEEP YOUR EYES OPEN. THE PUBLIC'S BEST DEFENSE IS A VIGILANT SOCIETY.

REALLY?

I THINK SO. I READ THAT ON A MAGNET ONCE.

As I sat on my beanbag, Batneezer became all serious and reminded me that I would still be visited by three more spirits tonight. He said that the first spirit would arrive when the clock struck one. The second at two and the third at—

Batneezer informed me that he would be popping in and out to teach me things that the other spirits couldn't. I thanked him for coming and for his concern. I then let him know that what I really wanted was to go to sleep and not think about anything that had to do with books or spirits for a little while. He didn't seem to care.

Batneezer began to dim and fade. He tried to
sound spookier than he was by whispering one last
line as he disappeared:

And with that, he was gone. I lay there wondering
about what I had just seen. It could have been a

ghost from my closet, or maybe it was a vision caused by indigestion from a bad bit of bread. I looked at my clock.

IT'S THE MIDDLE OF THE NIGHT. YOU SHOULD BE ASLEEP.

Before obeying my clock, I got out my copy of *A Christmas Carol* and read a few more pages. The story had been assigned in language arts, and I was almost done reading it. I liked it because it was short and I had seen so many movies about it that it felt familiar. I then pulled out a Batman comic from my drawer and looked at that. I knew I couldn't avoid the ghosts that were coming. I wanted to be as ready as possible.

Then I closed my eyes and drifted off to sleep.

CHAPTER 11

~

THE GHOST OF BOOKS PAST

At one o'clock, my alarm rang again even though I hadn't set it. I rolled over and shut it off. My room was dark, but there was a glowing light coming from my window. I jumped out of bed and went outside to take a look. I saw something shining behind the trees in the middle of the rock island.

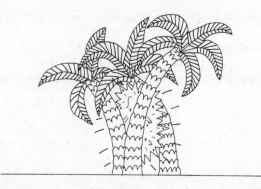

I don't advise people to get up in the middle of the night and walk toward a mysterious light, but that's exactly what I did. I thought it might be Jack messing around with his bug zapper, but as soon as I got closer, I could tell it was definitely not him.

HOW ARE YOU, MR. FUNNY FACE? BUUUURRRRRP! SORRY, PART OF ME IS VERY RUDE AND SMELLS LIKE MONKEY.

I was dumbfounded. First off, my face isn't funny. Second off, just what or who was I looking at? The ghost was a girl, and I wasn't positive what books she was inspired by. Part of her looked like Pippi

Longstocking with a monkey, while the other part just looked like a girl my age who could burp. I brushed my hair back and stood up straight. I suddenly wished I had put shorts on.

WHO ARE YOU?

I AM PIPPINANSTOCKING. IF YOU SAY IT FAST, IT'S FUNNY.

I'M NOT SURE I'LL BE SAYING IT AT ALL.

I looked around my neighborhood. It was one o'clock, and everyone was either asleep or inside their homes. I glanced back at my new visitor and wished Batneezer was there to tell me just who she was. Since he wasn't, I decided to ask for myself.

She didn't seem happy about my guess. She went on and on about how many volumes of books she was in and all the movies and TV shows that were about her. She also bragged about the complicated and interesting mysteries she had solved.

I could tell she was frustrated, but I really didn't know what books she was talking about. I also didn't want to guess and sound dumb. She took a deep breath and started talking.

I touched the end of her braid, and we began to float up over the palm trees. I had never traveled by braid, but it wasn't that bad. We headed back in the same direction Batneezer had taken me earlier. But instead of going to Softrock Middle School, we went to my old school, Curry Elementary. It was located directly across the street from Softrock. I had gone to Curry as a kid, but I hadn't been back since I finished sixth grade. We dropped down through the roof and right into Curry's school library. I wanted to be handling all of this like a brave person, but I don't think I was.

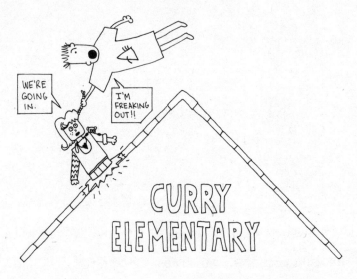

Once we were inside, everything looked familiar and comforting. The Ghost of Books Past started glowing brighter and lit up the place beautifully. When I was a little kid, I had spent a lot of time in this library, listening to the librarian read books and doing arts and crafts.

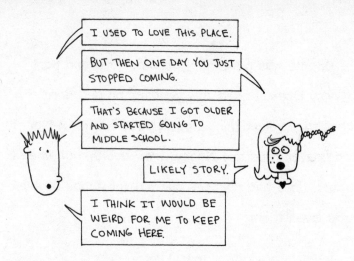

I USED TO LOVE THIS PLACE.

BUT THEN ONE DAY YOU JUST STOPPED COMING.

THAT'S BECAUSE I GOT OLDER AND STARTED GOING TO MIDDLE SCHOOL.

LIKELY STORY.

I THINK IT WOULD BE WEIRD FOR ME TO KEEP COMING HERE.

Pippiwhateverstocking was too busy thinking about something else to listen to me. She quickly led me over to a shelf where there was a long row of small books with yellow spines. She pointed to one and I pulled it out.

THAT'S ONE OF MY BOOKS.

NANCY DREW MYSTERY SERIES
THE SECRET OF THE OLD CLOCK

THE SECRET OF THE OLD CLOCK

OH, THAT OLD CLOCK.

So she was part Pippi Longstocking and part Nancy Drew. I liked the combination and decided that the coolest thing I could call her was P-Nan. I had never read any Nancy Drew books, but when I was little, I had checked one out for Janae because she loved them.

I had read a few Pippi Longstocking books when I was a kid. She was funny, and she lived in a house with no parents, and she had that monkey named Mr. Nilsson. What's not to like? Plus, she was super strong and could lift a horse.

I don't know exactly what she wanted me to feel, but if this library was to blame for turning me into a confused person with a crazy closet, then I wasn't too impressed.

Okay, I'll be honest—it was weird being back in my elementary school library. I had forgotten how much I loved some of the books I had read when I was a kid. You can't blame me for forgetting. It's really not something that kids my age stand around talking about anymore.

HEY, HAVE YOU SEEN THE NEW CLIFFORD? IT'S OUTSTANDING.

YEAH, IT'S ALMOST AS COOL AS THE LATEST ARTHUR.

CHECK OUT MY THOMAS TATTOO. IT'S TEMPORARY BUT MY LOVE FOR THOMAS ISN'T.

P-Nan told me that Beardy was worried about some of the things I had said about books. So she had come to show me the error of my ways. She had also come to right a wrong and needed me to look closely at the bookshelf. According to P-Nan, there was a book missing, and I was supposed to know where it was. I had no idea where it was or why she thought I had it. I also didn't think it was that big of a deal that one book was missing. P-Nan felt differently. She began to get very pushy and upset. She tried to pick up the entire bookcase, but because she was a ghost, she couldn't get a grip on it. She struggled for a few moments and then stopped to catch her breath. She counted to ten to calm down and then spoke.

THE POINT IS, YOU CHECKED OUT A COUPLE OF BOOKS YEARS AGO AND YOU NEVER BROUGHT THEM BACK.

I MIGHT HAVE CHECKED OUT SOME BOOKS WHEN I WAS A KID, BUT I'M SURE I RETURNED THEM AFTER NOT READING THEM.

WELL, YOU DIDN'T.

P-Nan was not happy with me. She stomped her ghost feet and tried to pick up the bookshelf again. As she was growling and throwing a fit, Batneezer appeared.

P-Nan took a few seconds to collect her thoughts. Once she was calm, she looked at me and smiled.

Then she disappeared in a flash of light. I looked at Batneezer, and he shrugged. I told him that he could have saved everyone a bunch of trouble by just giving me a few inspirational magnets instead. He said, "Bat, humbug," and instructed me to grab on to his waist. Batneezer pulled out a grappling gun and pointed it toward the ceiling.

Whoosh! We shot up through the roof and into the dark sky. We zipped along the ghostly string until we were above my house.

Batneezer dipped down through my window and dropped me onto my bed. He moved around my room in a huff and with clanking, and then as he left he once again used his exit as a chance to say something spooky:

In a flash, he was gone and I was alone in the dark once more. I looked at the clock.

STOP STARING AT MY FACE. IT'S ONE TWENTY-SEVEN.

If Batneezer was right, the next ghost would be showing up at two. I knew it was the middle of the night, but I was not going to go through all of this alone anymore. I put on some shorts and shoes and climbed through my window.

‹EXIT›

MY LIFE IS NUTS!

CHAPTER 12

RIGHTING A WRONG

It wasn't easy to wake Trevor. I had to tap on his window for almost five minutes before he finally popped up his tired head to *see* what was happening.

Jack was way easier to get because he was still awake in his room, melting crayons with his assault flashlight and a magnifying glass.

THE CRAYONS DISRESPECTED ME.

I didn't want to wake my other friends. It's not that I like Trevor and Jack more. It's just that . . . well, I guess I do like Trevor and Jack more. I quickly told them about Batneezer and what had happened with P-Nan.

YOU CALL HER P-NAN? WHY NOT PANCY?

OR PANCY-POO, LIKE NANCY DREW.

I told them how P-Nan had gotten mad at me because I had some books I had never returned. Trevor actually had a useful idea.

WE SHOULD ASK YOUR DOORKNOB. HE HAS ALL OF YOUR BOOKS LOCKED UP.

It was a good suggestion. I had never had a real conversation with Beardy, but his eyes could say a lot. He had to have some information. So we went back to my house, crawled in through my window as quietly as we could, and approached the infamous doorknob.

I NEED ANSWERS. ARE YOU HIDING SOME OVERDUE BOOKS?

Beardy didn't say anything. I asked him a few more questions and begged him a few more times to please tell me what I needed to do. He shut his eyes. I was about to give up on him when I saw something poking out under the bottom of the closet door.

I bent down and picked up two books—one was Pippi Longstocking, and the other was Nancy Drew. I had forgotten how long I had been throwing books into my closet. They both had CURRY ELEMENTARY stamped on the front page.

We took the dark alleys behind the house and in no time worked our way to Curry Elementary. There was a library book deposit on the side of the building, so I slipped the books in.

I turned my head and looked across the street toward Softrock Middle School. There was still one light on, and I could see Mr. Kerr's camper in the center of the parking lot. I huddled up with my friends and filled them in on how I had seen Mr. Kerr talking on the phone and acting suspicious earlier in the night.

We were all too curious to go home without investigating. Maybe it was the curiosity of Nancy Drew or the stubborn strength of Pippi, but I was up for finding out what was really going on. We crossed the street and approached our school. The front door was locked, so Jack suggested that we try to kick the doors down. Fortunately for us, someone had a better idea.

All three of us screamed as Batneezer spoke from behind us. I grabbed Jack so he didn't take off running, and we all stood staring at the ghost and trying to calm down. Once our heart rates were back to normal, I introduced them to Batneezer. Jack was the only one with a question.

I told Batneezer that we had been returning the lost books before we came over to check on Mr. Kerr. Batneezer graciously offered to help us get inside. Trevor and I pinched a sleeve while Jack took hold of the chain. Batneezer then floated straight toward the front door and right through it! When we got inside, he led us down the hall, past the art room, and into our school library. Mr. Kerr was sitting in front of one of the old computers. He couldn't see us. He was Skyping with a balding man with a big mouth.

WE'LL START THROWING OUT BOOKS THE DAY AFTER CHRISTMAS. THAT WAY, WHEN THE STUDENTS GET BACK FROM WINTER BREAK, THERE WILL BE NOTHING BUT COMPUTERS. AND THE COMPUTERS WON'T WORK UNLESS THEY PAY US EVEN MORE MONEY. WE'RE GOING TO MAKE A TON OFF OF THESE CHUMPS.

SOUNDS GREAT!

Trevor looked sick. He was a big fan of books, so hearing about them going away didn't sit well with him. As we listened, I was feeling ill. Mr. Kerr was a fraud. He was supposed to remodel our library and bring in some new computers, but now he was talking about getting rid of all the real books.

Jack reached out to smack Mr. Kerr in the back of the head, but his hand went right through him.

I didn't know what to do. It was obvious that Mr. Kerr was a crook and we had to stop him. But at the moment, we were just floating ghost kids, and he was a grown-up who had keys to the school and the trust of Principal Smelt.

Jack was *so* bothered that he let go of the chain. Suddenly, he was visible again. He looked at Mr. Kerr and made an awkward *yelp* noise as he fell to the floor.

Mr. Kerr jumped out of his seat and almost hit the ceiling in shock. Jack jumped up and took hold of Batneezer's chain, becoming invisible once more.

Mr. Kerr was sweaty and shaking. I was thinking about letting go myself so I could tie him up, but he looked so much stronger than me. Batneezer lifted his wrist and spoke into a small radio he had pulled from his belt.

Batneezer took out his grappling gun and shot it up through the ceiling again.

He ordered us to hold on tight and then we zipped up through the ceiling while Mr. Kerr was still looking around nervously and wondering about the surprise kid he had just seen. Trevor and Jack were both pretty happy about the whole flying thing.

I did like the flying part, but I was more concerned about what Mr. Kerr was going to do and how I could stop him. I wasn't scared, so I shut my eyes and tried to brainstorm.

LET'S START THINKING AND WORK THIS PROBLEM OUT.

CHAPTER 13

THE GHOST OF CHRISTMAS PRESENT

Batneezer dropped each of us off in our bedrooms.
I was the last to be taken home. After he let go of
me and before he faded, he said,

RECOMMENDED FOR AGES FIVE AND UP.

He was not very good at exit lines. I knew I was
tired, but there was no way I could actually sleep. I
looked at the clock.

YES, IT'S ONE FIFTY
IN THE MORNING.
AND YES, YOU
SHOULDN'T BE
AWAKE TO KNOW
THAT.

I fell asleep for fourteen minutes, but at 2:04,
something began tapping on my window. I was
surprised that my alarm hadn't gone off at 2:00. I
mean, I didn't set it, but it had been going off all
night. I got up and moved to the window.

IS THAT YOU,
BATNEEZER?

I pulled back the curtains and there was . . .
Trevor? He looked nervous.

I looked to the right of Trevor as the something
he was talking about stepped out from behind him
and started to glow. I stared at the visitor in
disbelief. It was probably the most obvious mash-up
I had ever seen and definitely the most familiar.

I loved Minecraft, and everyone under the sun played it. Now here was a part Creeper creeping in my front yard. The other part of the visitor resembled Greg Heffley from the Diary of a Wimpy Kid books. I quickly climbed out the window and took a closer look. He was creepy in a good way, so it made sense to call him that. Creepy told us both to take his hands. I grabbed the cartoon-drawn hand and was more than just a little freaked out. I had read all the Wimpy Kid books. Even when I hated reading, they seemed easy and super funny. Now I was holding Greg's hand.

I NEVER IMAGINED THIS EVER HAPPENING TO ME.

I DID!

The three of us shot through the air like a beam of light, and in less than a second, we were standing inside my middle school library again. I looked around, wondering if Mr. Kerr was there. He wasn't, just a lot of books.

WHAT ARE WE DOING HERE?

IT'S REALLY SAD THAT YOU DON'T KNOW.

I knew what a library was. I had been using my school library way more often these days. Some of the books I had read so I could figure out more about the creatures that had come from my closet. And a couple of days ago at lunch, I had even come into the library to read the assigned language arts book. I told the spirit this, and he said,

YEAH, YEAH—WE'RE ALL REAL IMPRESSED. NOW WHAT ARE YOU GOING TO DO WHEN THIS LIBRARY GOES AWAY?

Creepy looked sad. I knew he was talking about Mr. Kerr and how he was going to take all the books away and replace them with lame computers. It made sense that part of him would be sad, but the other part of him should have been okay with what was happening, because you can play Minecraft on some computers. When I mentioned this, he growled and there was a clicking noise that I recognized from playing the game. Now, right in front of me, there was a pixelated box of TNT.

Creepy walked over to a shelf that was filled with books about Minecraft. Like P-Nan, he wanted me to see how important he was and that he wasn't just a game. I wasn't too surprised that there were Minecraft books, because I read some myself when I was trying to get better at gaming. Also, Trevor had a ton of them at his house.

I picked a book off the shelf. It was one that I felt wouldn't make anyone a better person. I showed it to Creepy and asked him if he thought it would work.

He said it never hurts to be a little nicer. I told him that the wimpy part of him should probably read it, then. Creepy ignored me and went on and on about how spoiled Trevor and I were to have such an abundance of books to read. He also said it was extra important for me to be reading, because I was a writer. If I was writing down everything I was experiencing with the creatures from my closet, I had better fill my head with good examples. Because as he put it...

I DON'T WANT YOU TELLING OUR STORY LIKE A LAME-O.

Trevor started talking about how he was a writer too and how he was currently working on some fanfiction. His book was about what it would be like if R2-D2 was a real boy that looked just like him. Creepy tried to look interested, but finally he threw up his hands to stop Trevor.

We grabbed ahold of Creepy. He took me and
Trevor out through one of the school's walls and
toward the parking lot. We drifted over the pavement
and into Mr. Kerr's camper.

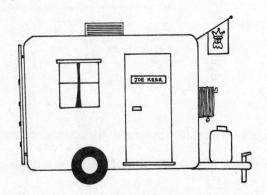

Inside, Mr. Kerr was sitting at a small table looking over a bunch of papers. He was laughing to himself about how smart he was and how much money he was going to make by ripping off our school. I studied the papers on his desk closely.

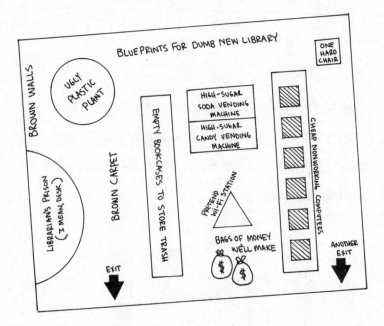

BLUEPRINTS FOR DUMB NEW LIBRARY

BROWN WALLS

UGLY PLASTIC PLANT

ONE HARD CHAIR

LIBRARIAN'S PRISON (I MEAN, DESK)

BROWN CARPET

EMPTY BOOKCASES TO STORE TRASH

HIGH-SUGAR SODA VENDING MACHINE

HIGH-SUGAR CANDY VENDING MACHINE

PRETEND WI-FI STATION

CHEAP NON-WORKING COMPUTERS

BAGS OF MONEY WE'LL MAKE

$ $

EXIT

ANOTHER EXIT

The blueprints for the new library were troubling. It didn't look like there would be books anymore. It made me a little sad to think about a library without *books*. I had been so mad at the Gwinnster and *books* that I had forgotten what was important. My heart felt sick.

I had asked the question with honest concern. He had answered with honest sarcasm. Sometimes Greg from *Diary of a Wimpy Kid* was snarky. Now, as he stood here mashed up with Creeper, his personality was still shining through. I needed answers.

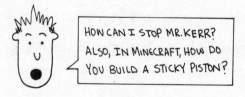

The creature told me everything I needed to know about building a sticky piston. He didn't give me specific ways to stop Mr. Kerr, but agreed that he was a big fart that needed to be stomped out and also said that Mr. Kerr was like a man who had the personality of stinky cheese. When Creepy was finished talking at us, he reached out his hands and told us it was time for him to go. We didn't want him to leave, but he insisted that . . .

We took his hands, and with a loud hiss and a pop, I was back in my bed and Trevor was gone.

Batneezer was floating at the end of the bed staring at me.

Batneezer insisted that, in time, I would have all the answers I needed. I thought it would be way easier if he would just tell me the answers, but he insisted that he didn't believe in charity. I then insisted that I had no idea what he was talking about. Batneezer didn't try to explain; he just began to fade away and threw out another one of his dramatic and confusing exit lines.

THE BATMOBILE GETS BAD GAS MILEAGE.

I was confused—not about the Batmobile's gas mileage—I was confused because this night was lasting forever, and it was not the way I had planned it to go. I also was bummed because I would have liked to have a little more time with Creepy. I had a few more questions about Minecraft. I also wanted to know the answer to Trevor's question about Fregley, but Creepy was gone and so was Batneezer.

I lay back on my bed and stared at the ceiling. Then I looked in Beardy's direction. It was dark, so I couldn't see him. I thought about using my flashlight, but it must have rolled under my bed and it would take too much effort to get it. So I struck up a dark conversation with my doorknob.

As I was talking to him and pouring out my tired heart, my alarm clock rang again.

CHAPTER 14

GETTING SERIOUS

I hit my clock to stop the alarm and sat up anxiously. I had seen the Ghost of Books Past, the Ghost of Present-Day Books, and if the book was right, I was about to meet the Ghost of Books Yet to Come. I didn't have to wonder long if it would happen.

This new visitor wasn't glowing like the others had. In my dark room, I couldn't *see* him at all. I could only hear his deep voice.

I AM THE GHOST OF BOOKS YET TO COME.

I THINK I FEAR YOU THE MOST.

WHY?

BECAUSE I STILL STRUGGLE WITH READING SOMETIMES.

THAT MAKES SENSE.

It was uncomfortable not being able to see him. But at least the dark hid the fact that I was shivering and nervous. I swallowed my fears and asked him where he would be taking me and how we would travel there. His answer was disappointing.

UM, WE'RE JUST GOING INTO YOUR LIVING ROOM. I THOUGHT WE'D WALK.

OH.

The Ghost of Books Yet to Come told me to open my bedroom door and instructed me to go down the hall. I slowly walked past him. I still couldn't clearly see who or what he was because the rest of the house was almost as dark as my room. I moved out into our family room and near the Christmas tree.

GHOST OF BOOKS YET TO COME, WHAT ARE WE DOING IN MY LIVING ROOM? I DON'T WANT TO WAKE UP MY FAMILY. ALSO, I CAN'T SEE A THING.

The Ghost of Books Yet to Come informed me that my family couldn't hear anything that was happening. He said that the sound and sight of ghosts was something only I and the people they wanted to bother could hear. I complained some more about the dark, and suddenly the Christmas tree lights began to glow. They lit up the room in a dull light, revealing a terrifying new spirit creature.

Unholy spookony! I didn't know whether I should
scream or run. I thought about doing both, but I
knew that this visitor would find me. I couldn't see
the ghost's face, but he stood there towering over
me! He motioned to the gifts beneath our
Christmas tree. I saw he was pointing at a couple of
presents with my name on them. They were gifts
from my grandparents. I picked up one of them and
knew instantly from the weight and feel that it was
a book.

My heart sank. I know it's shallow of me to say this, but I don't love getting books as gifts. Sure, books are great, I'll admit that, but holiday gifts are for paintball guns and cell phones.

The Ghost of Books Yet to Come took a few
moments to lecture me about how important it was
to be grateful for what you are given and to
appreciate *books* like they should be appreciated.
He was getting a little preachy, but I decided not to
point that out because he still frightened me. He
reached down and handed me the other book-
shaped gift.

TELL ME SPIRIT, ARE
THESE BOOKS I'LL LIKE?
ARE THEY GREAT FANTASY
ADVENTURES?

The Ghost of Books Yet to Come shook his head.

THEY'RE AT LEAST FICTION, RIGHT?

The ghost shook his head again. I begged him to
tell me what they were, then. He pulled off his hood
and said very dramatically,

NONFICTION!

I let out a scream! It was one thing for me to read *books* that were funny and exciting, but nonfiction sort of scared me. When I thought of nonfiction I thought of *books* like . . .

SOMETHING BORING HAPPENED

AND NOW YOU HAVE TO READ ABOUT IT

BY ED SNOOZE

EXTRA THICK EDITION

EVEN THE SPINE IS BORING

I looked at the Ghost of Books Yet to Come and tried to stop shaking. I couldn't figure out what was

happening. He was definitely nonfiction and scary
looking. He was also super messed up. He had wild
hair and a tall stovepipe hat. He had a beard and
a half mustache and two uneven eyes. I had gotten
pretty good about guessing what books inspired
the creatures from my closet, but I wasn't sure
about this one. So I asked him outright. His answer
didn't help.

I stared at him, racking my brain to figure out
what the heck that meant. I guess he could see how
confused I was, because he said,

I was impressed. It was kinda cool to have parts of Abe and Albert in my house. I'm pretty sure they were a couple of the smartest people ever. So I gave them a really smart-sounding name: Abe-ert. I felt kind of uneasy about the whole situation and the heaviness of the night. I told Abe-ert that, but he just kept going on and on about energy and emancipation—two e words I needed to learn more about. He was super smart. I was about to sit down on the couch when Batneezer appeared to save the day.

They argued for a few minutes before Abe-ert promised not to make fun of fiction if Batneezer would acknowledge the importance of nonfiction. Batneezer agreed, and the fighting stopped. I sighed in relief while we stood there looking at each other. Finally, I asked Batneezer what we were supposed to do next.

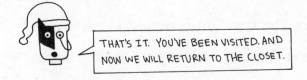

THAT'S IT. YOU'VE BEEN VISITED. AND NOW WE WILL RETURN TO THE CLOSET.

What?! I had a small fit and reminded Batneezer about Mr. Kerr, and how he wanted to destroy our library, and how he had to be stopped. I couldn't allow him to do such a horrible thing to our school. Not when I had access to some pretty interesting ghosts. I needed the ghosts of books past, present, and future to help me scare Mr. Kerr away.

I explained to Batneezer and Abe-ert what I wanted them to do and how things were going to go down. They liked the plan and disappeared in a flash. The tree lights snapped off as they left, leaving the living room dark. I felt my way back to my room and climbed out my window to fetch Trevor and Jack. I wasn't sure if they would be of any help, but I knew they would at least want to witness what was about to happen.

CHAPTER 15

SOFTROCK ASYLUM

Trevor, Jack, and I were behind the bushes, staring out at Mr. Kerr's camper in the school parking lot. It was almost four o'clock in the morning now. We were all tired. I personally would have loved to be home sleeping. After all, it was Christmas Eve, and we were crouching in the dirt waiting for ghosts.

There wasn't much of a plan. Batneezer and his friends were going to scare the bad out of Mr. Kerr by appearing to him inside of his camper. Hopefully, he would be so shaken up that he would leave our school and never hurt another library again. Our job was to wait for the Bat-Signal. Then we were going to run around and pound on the side of the camper to add dramatic scare.

As we were crouched behind the bushes, Batneezer appeared right next to us. We all jumped and screamed more than we should have. I don't care who you are, you never get used to ghosts just popping up. Batneezer was supposed to be in the camper scaring Mr. Kerr, so it was extra surprising to see him behind the bushes. When I had settled down, I asked him why he was there.

THE OTHER SPIRITS AND I ARE JUST ABOUT TO BEGIN SCARING MR. KERR. I JUST WANTED TO LET YOU KNOW THAT I BROUGHT A FEW EXTRA FRIENDS.

EXTRA FRIENDS? WHAT ARE YOU TALKING ABOUT?

Batneezer didn't answer. He just disappeared in a flash. I started to say something, but I was interrupted by someone grabbing the back of my shirt and pulling me up. Whoever it was was also lifting up Jack. I started to scream and kick, but it was too strong. Trevor could have run off, since he wasn't being held, but that would have been rude.

Mr. Kerr came out of his camper in the middle
of the parking lot and looked in our direction. I
knew he was planning to ruin our library, but suddenly
he was the only help we could see. Trevor began to
yell politely, but Mr. Kerr didn't do anything. The
man holding us by our collars pushed us across
the parking lot and right toward Mr. Kerr. Trevor
was trying to help by making suggestions in the
kindest way possible.

We were shoved up to the trailer, where Mr. Kerr was standing with his hands on his hips. He didn't look like he wanted to help us. He called the man holding us Dave and asked what was going on. We tried to act like it was all just a big mistake and that we were minding our own business hiding behind the bushes at four in the morning, but they weren't buying it. Trevor then tried to smooth things out by using some of the communication skills he had learned in Pleasant Scouts.

Mr. Kerr kept looking at Jack. Jack stared right back at him. The two of them exchanged glances for a moment before Mr. Kerr spoke.

WAIT A SECOND, I THINK I SAW THIS KID IN THE LIBRARY EARLIER TONIGHT. JUST WHAT ARE YOU PUNKS UP TO?

I thought about keeping my mouth shut, but I was mad at Mr. Kerr for what he was going to do to our library. I also didn't like being called a punk. It was a word old people used to describe young people they didn't understand. Sure, I probably would have kept my mouth shut a few months ago, but I had been through so many things with the creatures that I couldn't keep it shut now. So I opened it and told him everything.

WE KNOW YOUR EVIL PLAN. YOU'RE GOING TO RUIN OUR LIBRARY AND TAKE MONEY FROM OUR SCHOOL. WE KNOW EVERYTHING.

WELL, THAT'S TOO BAD.

Mr. Kerr and Dave began talking and complaining to each other about how me and my punk friends were going to ruin everything. While he held me by the back of my shirt, I wondered where Batneezer was and tried to look around. He had promised he was going to help, and now here we were, helpless. Mr. Kerr tried reasoning with us.

LISTEN, KIDS, THIS IS ALL JUST A BIG MISTAKE.

He told us how he and Dave were going to get our school new computers and how much better the library would be. He then offered us all a little money if we would be smart enough to keep quiet and not mention that we saw him tonight.

HOW MUCH MONEY?

I didn't know what to do. I couldn't just go home and not say anything. Mr. Kerr and Dave were crooks! He kept trying to bribe us. Then he said something I just couldn't let slide.

BESIDES, WHO NEEDS BOOKS? YOU KIDS HAVE BETTER THINGS TO DO THAN READ.

I clenched my fists and growled. I could feel my neck growing red and my ears beginning to steam. I was just about ready to speak my mind when something swooped down out of the dark sky and flashed right through Mr. Kerr. He screamed and swatted at the air as if he was walking through a cobweb.

It was Batneezer! He swooped back around and then appeared as bright as he could directly in front of us. Trevor clapped while Mr. Kerr looked on in stunned disbelief. To make things even more interesting, Creepy and Abe-ert and P-Nan showed up too. They all glowed as brightly as they could and had changed things so Mr. Kerr and Dave could now actually see them.

Dave let go of us and grabbed Jack's flashlight. He swung it as hard as he could at Batneezer, but the flashlight went right through him. Dave smiled a wicked smile.

I had no idea what Batneezer meant by reinforcements. If he was talking about me and my friends, then we were in trouble. Happily, I didn't have to worry about it for too long because Batneezer whistled and I heard noises coming from the direction of Mr. Kerr's camper. I looked over, and there, standing on the top, was one of the best sights I had ever seen.

Batneezer had somehow gotten my closet door open. And now the five creatures I had been visited by in the past were here to help me again! Pinocula, Potterwookiee, Seussol, Katfish, and Wonkenstein!

They jumped from the roof and rained down on Mr. Kerr and Dave.

WATCH THE HAIR! WATCH THE HAIR!

Batneezer and the others began to swarm, hollering and moaning. Mr. Kerr opened the door of his camper and tried to get inside.

Trevor, Jack, and I stood there in awe. It was like the perfect storm of ghosts and creatures and books. It would have been cool to just sit back and watch, but we all wanted in on the action.

Jack picked up his flashlight and began shining it on people as Trevor kicked at Dave's ankles while he was attempting to fight off Seussol. Just then, Katfish yelled for us to throw her the extension cords hanging on the front of the camper. I didn't know why she wanted them, but we did as we were told. We grabbed them and tossed them over to her and Wonk.

THANKS!

If my life was normal, I would have been at home sleeping. Maybe there would have been visions of sugarplums dancing in my head. But my life wasn't normal, and because of that, I was in my school

parking lot on Christmas Eve morning taking down
two thugs who were trying to harm my school. It
was a noisy, wild scene that reminded me of
something out of the old Batman shows my dad
had showed me.

It didn't take that long for good to triumph over
bad. In just a few minutes, we had Mr. Kerr and

Dave tied up to the back of the camper and begging for mercy.

Some of the houses near the school had heard the kerfuffle and called the police. The sirens in the distance were getting nearer.

I remembered from *A Christmas Carol* that lots of people owed Scrooge money. But after being visited by the ghosts, he saw the light and forgave their debts. So in the spirit of Scrooge, I did the same. It was super easy, seeing how I owed all the creatures from my closet much more than they owed me. I then thanked them for changing my life in a good way.

I wanted to hang out and ask a ton of questions, but the police sirens were getting louder and Batneezer insisted that it was their time to go.

I looked at Trevor and Jack, hoping one of them would speak up and stop them from leaving. But Trevor was crying and Jack was poking Dave with his flashlight. The sirens grew ever louder, and I knew that if the creatures didn't leave, I would have a whole new set of problems to deal with. Trevor suggested one last hug.

Then Batneezer and the other spirits disappeared while the rest of the creatures took off into the dark. My friends and I stayed where we were as the cops pulled into the parking lot. We explained what had happened and how we alone had tied up Mr. Kerr and Dave. We told them about what Mr. Kerr was going to do to our school and how the evil master plans were inside. The cops didn't believe us at first, but when they searched the camper, they found all they needed to prove that Mr. Kerr and Dave were bad guys. Mr. Kerr began hollering.

... THERE WERE GHOSTS AND A MONKEY AND A GIRL SOCKED ME IN THE STOMACH AND A PUPPET BIT ME!

The cops arrested them both and then they drove us to our houses. Just so you know, it's never easy to wake your parents early in the morning and tell them the cops want to speak with them.

The cops told my parents that I was a hero. They had to say it twice for my parents to believe them.

After the police left, I wanted to go to bed, but unfortunately it was morning and I had a paper route. My adventure had been a bit different than Scrooge's. Actually, a lot different. In the book, the spirits had come on Christmas Day, but now it was just Christmas Eve morning. The spirit creatures had done it all in one night. We had saved my school and gotten rid of some bad people, but I still had to deliver the papers.

It was truly a Christmas miracle! I ran to my room before they could change their minds.

CHAPTER 16

ALL'S WELL THAT ENDS WELL

Christmas morning was fun. It probably sounds selfish to list the gifts first, but Tuffin got everything he wanted. Libby and I, on the other hand, got some of the things we asked for. My parents gave me a couple of video games and a couple of books and new pants that I was never going to wear.

Let's just say I liked getting the books about Abraham Lincoln and Einstein much better than getting the pants. After opening our gifts, we made a ton of food and played board games. We then went on a family walk, which sounds lame, but it was actually pretty fun.

The truth is, I hardly remember Christmas because the next week of my life was so crazy. The *Temon Times* ran a big article about me and Trevor and Jack. It talked about how we had stopped some criminals from harming our school and had saved our library.

Everyone in the town of Temon thought we were heroes. It turned out that Mr. Kerr and Dave had done bad things to schools in seven other states. They were behind bars now and no longer a threat to libraries. Aaron, Rourk, and Teddy were really jealous and mad that I hadn't included them in our heroics.

Everyone in Temon sent me and Trevor and Jack books to thank us for what we had done—even the mayor! All kinds of books about all kinds of stories

and people. My room and house were stacked with
them. We had lost my little brother twice in the
piles.

I had a feeling that Abe-ert would be pretty
happy if he could see all the books that were going
to be a part of my future.

I still hadn't seen Batneezer or any other
creature since they had left us in the school parking
lot. And to make things even stranger, my closet
was no longer locked. I could open the door and see
how messy it was. When I used the tool Seussol

gave me to see when the next creature would visit, Beardy wouldn't open. He just sat there smiling.

Janae and I exchanged gifts the day after Christmas. I gave her a necklace with a heart on it. I had worried about my gift being too sappy, but when she kissed me after I gave it to her, I felt differently.

Janae also promised that to make up for me missing her party, she was going to invite me over to watch a movie and eat popcorn with just her. I liked that idea a lot. Then, as if she wasn't already amazing enough, she gave me my gift, and I was blown away by it. I didn't think that Janae knew about my Thumb Buddy collection, but Tuffin had told her and she had found one for me. It was the rare Hulk Thumb Buddy from the A-pin-ger series. It was rare because they had mistakenly put two mouths on it and left off the nose.

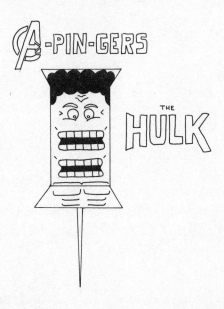

Not only did Janae not make fun of me for collecting such embarrassing things, but she also told me she thought it was cute. It was a winter break that I will never forget.

EPILOGUE

I'm not sure what to write here. I mean, what do I put down that would properly say all the things I want to say? I started keeping a journal many months ago, when Wonk came. At that time, I wanted nothing to do with books. Now I am surrounded by them. I guess I've changed. I know it was books that helped change me the most. And even though every day of my life won't be perfect, I'm pretty happy about the future.

The last day of winter break, Trevor and Jack loaded up some of the duplicate copies of books we had been given and donated them to our school. We might not be getting a new library, but the school would now have tons of new books.

We rolled down the road like a street gang with a

desire for reading. Sometimes the best endings are the ones filled with wheelbarrows of possibility.

THE END

OBERT SKYE

**What sparked your imagination for *Batneezer*?
Why did you choose to cross Batman and Ebenezer
Scrooge? Who are you more like: Batman or Ebenezer
Scrooge? Why?**
My imagination is constantly sparking—life just does that to
me. But sparking my imagination was easy with *Batneezer.*
A Christmas Carol is one of my favorite stories of all time—
it's imaginative, spooky, and comes with a few emotional
punches. Scrooge is such a horrible and wonderful charac-
ter. He felt like the perfect fit for Lego Batman—seeing how
I have a deep love for Legos—and clicking those two characters together made a lot of sense to me.

**Batneezer is the final book in the Creature from My
Closet series. What is the biggest challenge of ending
a series? What is the most rewarding part?**
This book was so much fun to write. Not only do you get
Batneezer, but there are a bunch of other bonus mash-ups
who appear in the last adventure. I've written a number of
"last books" in series and they are always the hardest. I
want to make sure that the story makes everyone excited to
see what comes to pass. When it works, like I think it does in

Batneezer, it's rewarding to see those characters "stick the landing" and bring their story to a fitting end.

You're both the author and illustrator of many books you create. How do you first conceive of your characters? Do you start by drawing or writing?

For the books I illustrate I almost always begin by writing the character. I like to use words to draw them up in my mind. Then I use those images to help shape their comic forms on the page. Rob, however, has been in my head for so long that I feel I've always known who he is and how he looks. For the creatures, I take my time drawing a bunch of ideas and finding the right look and combination.

You visit lots of schools around the country to meet your readers. What is your favorite part of school visits?

I love visiting schools! I have been lucky to travel to so many places I would never have gone had it not been for the connection made between my books and students. It's very cool getting to meet so many readers and hearing what they think about books in general, and my writing specifically. It really makes the world seem huge and small, all at the same time. I hope I get the chance to talk about the Creature from My Closet books for many years to come. Rob's closet is one amazing place.

If you heard a strange rattling sound in your closet and discovered a mythical creature there, what's the first thing you would do?

Duck behind my bed and scream. Actually, I'd probably scream and then duck.

SQUARE FISH

Who is your favorite fictional character and why?
Willy Wonka. I like how odd he is and that he owns a chocolate factory. My goal is to have my own chocolate factory someday. I want to be like Willy.

Who or what did you most like to doodle when you were young?
I liked to doodle everything. Weird animals were my favorite subjects. I did a comic strip for my school called *Prep-punker*. It was about a goofy, preppy punk rocker. It was kind of my beginning in telling stories with pictures.

What kind of books did you enjoy most when you were young?
I loved anything funny and exciting. Those were my two favorite types of books to read then and now. I loved when a book made me laugh and caused my heart to beat fast. I always try to make my books have a lot of humor and exciting things happening in them.

Society may be in danger, but
middle school must go on.

OBERT SKYE

GEEKED
OUT

A LAME NEW WORLD

Keep reading for an excerpt.

CHAPTER ONE
The Ruin

The world is coming to an end. Or maybe it's just a phase—it's hard to tell. Things could smooth out in a couple of hundred years, but at the moment things are a mess, and the worst of it is that we still have to go to school. Seriously, if you think your school is hard, try going to one when society has fallen apart.

How did the world fall apart? Well, I'm glad I asked that. To begin with, things weren't going well all over the planet. Governments were fighting about things that they thought mattered, and people were polluting places that they thought didn't matter. People were unhappy and society and technology seemed to be getting out of hand. Then, as if things weren't tough enough, something happened that unraveled everything. You see, there are some very, very, very popular books called the Sand Thrower series.

The books are about a boy and a girl who travel through time by throwing sand and occasionally kissing. I'm not a huge fan, but almost all the girls (and a ton of boys) are obsessed with them.

A few years ago the Sand Thrower movie franchise released their third movie, *Grainy*. The first two movies were really good and kids loved them. But, the third movie blew chunks. I mean, it really stunk—like a dead skunk that's been sprayed with my grandmother's perfume and rolled in bad eggs. It was the best book in the series, but they made it into the worst movie ever! Because it stunk so bad, society went bonkers. Fans all over the world left the theaters and took to the streets. They tore things up. Not even the cops could stop people from weeping and interrupting society with their sad selfies and uncontrollable behavior.

It was the beginning of the end.

The nonstop texting and online complaining caused hundreds of communications satellites to drop out of orbit and come crashing to earth. The failed satellites did massive amounts of damage and helped throw society into the toilet for many months. Governments couldn't communicate, people started more wars, and all systems experienced breakdowns. Factories and fires pumped out waste and smoke that made the weather bonkers. Everything fell apart, and the whole world changed—countries crumbled, states went to pieces, and neighborhoods got picked apart.

It was the end of one world and the start of another.

Now the government is bigger, and our streets are ruled by packs of unhappy, unsatisfied, and pushy fangirls and fanboys that society calls Fanatics. Most Fanatics spend their days silently stewing and aggressively taking selfies. Some attack people in outfits they don't like or chase down anyone who dares to say the third Sand Thrower movie is better than the book.

It's crazy. Middle school is hard enough, but add the breakdown of society to the daily grind, and it gets even stickier. I shouldn't complain too much. At least I'm lucky to be part of a group at school. The group I'm talking about is the AV Club. It used to stand for Audio Visual Club, but now it stands for Avoid Violence Club, because that's what we spend most of our day doing. We're thinkers, not fighters, and there are four of us: me, Mindy, Owen, and Xennitopher.

Tip   Mindy   Owen   Xen

Owen is older than all of us by almost half a year. He has about a dozen people in his family and doesn't like to go home because his big brothers pick on him. He doesn't like to do things that are hard because it makes his skin turn red and his nose run. He's kind and also kind of slow moving. According to the school aptitude test we had to take a few weeks ago, he would be best suited in a job where he didn't have to interact with others.

Xennitopher is my brother from another mother. He is

probably the coolest member of the AV Club. His hair always looks perfect, and he knows how to code in four languages. I've also seen him lift things that look heavy. His dad works for the mayor of Piggsburg and his mother works at the zoo protecting the animals from poachers.

Don't tell anyone, but Mindy is my favorite. We sort of have a thing. I mean, she sort of likes me as a friend. She was born in Japan and moved to Piggsburg shortly before the world unraveled. She is the glue in the AV Club. And not the cheap kind of glue they use at our school, but the kind of glue that could adhere a steam train to a steel rail. She's incredibly smart, and I wouldn't be surprised if someday we got married.

My name is Timothy Dover, but everyone calls me Tip, as in Tip Dover. It works because sometimes I have a hard time standing up without tripping. I used to mind the nickname, but now I'm fine with it and even kind of like it. I am an only child, and I have never fit in other than in the AV Club. Which is strange, because I'm a Fourth Master Elf in the *Elf Scrimmage* role-playing game, and you would think that would get me some respect, but it doesn't.

Our school is called Otto Waddle Jr. High Government Outpost, but we all call it WADD. The nickname works because our mascot is a weird wad-shaped creature, plus the school itself is a large wad of confusion.

Because my friends and I have high IQs, most of the school calls us Geeks and they give us a ton of grief. I guess being smart at WADD is uncool. I don't know which one of us Geeks is the smartest, but I was the only one who could figure out how to open the lid on Owen's asthma medicine.

BREATHE RIGHT PILLS

Twist twice to the left and once to the right. Squeeze bottle and throw bottle against the wall. Do not take if sleeping. Sing a song about kittens. But say your name out loud and then shake like a rattle.

Also, I got an A, plus a handful of rice, in yesterday's Identifying Edible Weeds class. It was an important test. You might not be aware of this, but knowing the difference between edible and inedible things can save your life.

DANDELION   BAMBOO   SHRIMP AND PEA
                               FLAVORED RAMEN

Eat   Eat   DO NOT EAT

THE CREATURE FROM MY CLOSET

WHAT CREATURE WILL
COME OUT OF ROB'S CLOSET NEXT?

mackids.com

SQUARE FISH